INSIDE THE EGG

A SEVEN WARDENS STORY

SKYE MACKINNON
LAURA GREENWOOD

Peryton Press

THE SEVEN WARDENS SERIES

1. From the Deeps (Audiobook Available)
2. Into the Mists (Audiobook Available)
3. Beneath the Earth
4. Within the Flames
5. Above the Waves
6. Under the Ice
7. Rule the Dark

- Through the Storms (optional spin-off between books 1 & 2)
- Below the Baubles (optional short story between books 5 & 6)
- Beyond the Loch (optional novella set before the events of the Seven Wardens series)
- Inside the Egg (novella set after book 7)
- Seven Wardens Boxed Set: Books 1-4
- Seven Wardens Boxed Set: Books 5-7

BLURB

Macey thought she was done saving the world…she was wrong.

When Amber uncovers an egg that could destroy the world, Macey and the other Wardens are drawn into a race against time to defeat the evil lurking inside the egg.
Can they give in to the egg's demands? Or is there a way to restore balance to the world without giving in?

Inside The Egg is a HEA story for the splashingly good fantasy reverse harem series, Seven Wardens.

THE SEVEN WARDENS

Water: Macey (Kelpie)
Wind: Cam (Wraith)
Fire: Flint (Wraith)
Earth: Jared (Incubus)
Ice: Izban (Mage)
Lightning: Amber (Beithir)
Air: Talia (Seelie hosted within Macey)

Their Companions

Lucien (Daimon)
Rónán (Selkie)
Nessie (Kelpie)

To all the people looking for comfort in things that are familiar to them right now.
We understand, we just wrote this instead of the things we were supposed to be doing (and have zero regrets).

1

Macey stared at the giant golden egg in her hands.

"And you're sure this is a dragon egg?" she asked Amber, who was grinning at Macey's stunned expression.

"Izban promised. He knows how much I miss having pets."

Macey choked. "You're going to have a dragon as a pet?"

"Hey, you have five guys to keep you company. Sometimes, Izban just isn't cuddly enough."

The beithir was right about that. Macey was constantly kept busy by her partners. They either wanted something from her, or decided she was in need of attention. Not that she complained. She loved them, each and every one. Cam and Flint, both wraiths but as different as day and night. Jared, the passionate incubus. Ronan, her gentle selkie. And Luc, the daimon who'd given up everything for her. She was truly blessed. Even if she sometimes missed having some alone time.

"How big is it going to get?" she asked her friend.

"Well, I guess dragon-big? But dragons live for centuries, so I assume they grow quite slowly."

"You assume? There's a lot of guesswork going on."

Amber shrugged. "I'm planning to go to the library soon to find something on dragon husbandry. There has to be a guide somewhere. How else would people know how to raise dragons?"

Macey cocked her head to the side and studied her best friend. Was she being serious? A dragon sounded like a lot of trouble, even for a girl who could shift into what was ultimately a giant flying snake. And if Macey had learned anything from her adventures, it was that most things weren't what they seemed on the outside. And almost all of them were more dangerous.

"Why don't I come with you?" she suggested. She had plenty of time, with her men busy doing their own thing.

Jared was still asleep, completely sated from last night's activities and in some kind of incubus stupor. Flint and Cam were off running errands, while Luc visited his mother, and Ronan was doing...

She frowned. She didn't actually *know* what Ronan was doing, but she hadn't seen him in a few hours.

Amber squealed with delight. "Yes, it'll be just like old times."

"Without half the maiming, death, and destruction," Macey muttered.

"Oh, I don't know. Life can get boring sometimes."

Amber set the egg down and grabbed her coat from the cupboard in front of them. One that hadn't been there moments before. Just one of the many advantages that came from living in the house in the mists. Not many people had the advantage of a house that provided everything they needed, when they needed it.

"If you want to go back to saving the world, that's fine by me," Macey said. "But don't go taking me with you."

"Are you telling me that if a phoenix started burning down houses everywhere, you wouldn't go along and Water Warden all over it?" Amber asked sweetly.

Macey chuckled. "Water Warden all over it?"

"You know, pssssshoe pssssshoe, water spurts out of your hands." Amber flung her arms up to explain.

"And you couldn't think of a better way to describe that?"

"Nope. Now, get your coat on. We're going to the library." She leaned into the cupboard and pulled Macey's coat out before handing it to her.

"The Staran will put us right outside the library, we probably don't need coats," Macey pointed out even as she put it on.

Amber narrowed her eyes dramatically. "I don't trust them."

"They're fixed now," Macey promised.

"Let's call it residual fear then." Amber shrugged. "But I like being prepared." She slipped the egg into her bag.

"You're not bringing it with us, are you?" Macey's

eyes widened as she considered what a colossally bad idea that was. There was no doubt in her mind that it would end badly. Probably with a dragon trying to destroy the library or something similar to that.

"Of course. What if it hatches while I'm gone? I don't want it to be on its own."

"I'm sure it could look after itself," Macey muttered. "And what happens to it once you and Izban have a child of your own?" She'd almost said egg rather than child, but caught herself in time. Who knew what the child of a beithir and a mage would come out like.

The redhead's cheeks flamed, almost matching her hair in colour. "That's not happening yet."

"But you said yourself that the dragon would..."

"Let's go," Amber insisted, cutting her off. "And if you continue, I'll start mentioning kids in front of Flint again. You know how desperate he is to be a father."

Macey sighed. "Fine." She wasn't ready, and Flint knew that, but it wouldn't stop the yearning in his eyes, and she didn't want to put him through that again.

Now that the world was safe - well, as safe as it ever would be with how destructive humans were - they had finally been able to settle down in their house in the mists. Macey loved having her own home again. As much as she missed the loch she'd grown up in, there was nothing better than sharing a house with her men, safe in the knowledge that nobody was out to kill them, and that they wouldn't have to leave in order to save the world once again.

She still visited the loch twice a week at least to

check on things. Even though she'd passed on her rule to her cousin, the kelpies still saw her as a leader.

"Come on," Amber said impatiently, tugging on Macey's arm. "I don't want to get there to find the library closed."

Macey smiled at her friend's enthusiasm. Sometimes, Amber seemed younger than she was. More innocent. She hoped the beithir would keep that innocence for as long as possible.

They stepped out of the house where the mists welcomed them with their familiar aniseed scent. Macey breathed in deep, then raised her arms to summon the Staran. It had become second nature to her, especially now that the magical pathways were healed and fully functional again. No more ending up in places she didn't want to, unless the Staran decided she was needed there. That hadn't happened in a long time though.

The Staran spat them out in a narrow alley around the corner from the British Library in London, just like Macey had asked. It was always better to arrive out of sight where humans couldn't see them appear out of thin air. Most people would ignore them, thinking it had been a trick of the light, but there were those who were naturally prone to believe in the supernatural.

They entered the library and headed straight down the stairs to the magical section. It was invisible to human eyes, but Macey had been here before and knew the way. A kabouter female was sitting at the reception desk, immersed in a dusty volume full of strange scribblings that Macey couldn't identify.

"Hi," Amber greeted her cheerily. "Do you have any books about dragons? Specifically dragon husbandry?"

"Shelf 4b," the librarian said without looking up. "And beware the bookworms, they're out in force today."

It took them a while to find shelf 4b, mostly because it wasn't between 4a and 4c as you would have expected. The magical library was nothing but mysterious.

There were a surprising amount of books on dragons. Amber pulled half a dozen from the shelf.

"Look, that one is a guide to dragon eggs! I wonder if it will help me identify what kind of dragon will hatch from mine. And, wow, that book is about training your dragon for battle. How cool is that."

Macey chuckled. "I'll do the dragon egg identification, you look for something that will actually teach you how to look after a baby dragon."

Reluctantly, Amber handed her the book and pulled out the egg so that Macey could compare it with the pictures.

As soon as Macey opened the book, she regretted her offer. There were hundreds of different dragon species. She'd assumed there might be a handful, maybe twenty at most, but no. According to the book, there were three hundred and fifty known kinds of dragon. The introduction went as far as to say that if hybrids were included, the total would be more like six hundred different species.

Macey sighed and went to work. This was going to take a while.

She looked up to see where Amber had got to, but her friend was already down the next row of shelves. Macey shook her head and smiled to herself. When the beithir set her mind to something, it was almost impossible to get her off track. Macey had no idea how Izban dealt with it. The Ice Warden was notably grumpy about everything in his life, except for his girlfriend.

She pulled her mind away from her friend's love life and flicked through the book. None of the dragon eggs looked remotely like the one in Amber's bag.

Perhaps she was mistaken about what it looked like. She turned to the egg and examined it. The golden shell glinted in the dim lighting of the library. Why didn't they have better lighting in here? Was it to protect the books? Because if the bookworms were anything to go by, there wasn't much hope for them.

Macey's concentration was ripped away from the egg when Amber let out a short scream. Macey was on her feet within seconds. Time might have passed since the Wardens had been saving the world, but that didn't mean her instincts had faded.

She set the egg down, wincing as it clunked against the table. There was no time to check it was alright. She was certain dragons must have strong shells, it wouldn't make sense otherwise.

With her hands freed, Macey set off to help her friend. She'd not spent too much time in the British Library, but she wouldn't be surprised to learn that nasty things lived here.

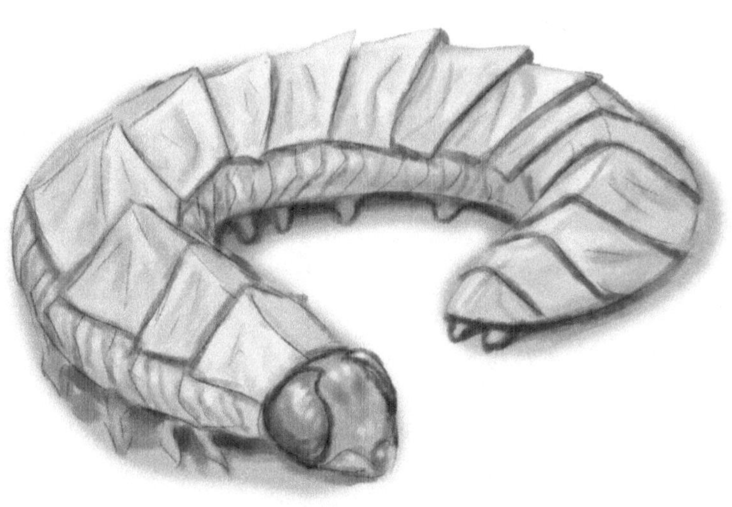

2

Macey called water magic into her hands, readying herself to attack whatever it was that hurt her friend. She didn't want anything to happen to Amber; they'd been through far too much for that. She turned the corner and entered the row of books the beithir had disappeared behind.

It took a moment for the sight in front of her to register, but when it did, she sighed with relief.

Amber was sprawled across the floor, with books all around her, something squirming in her hands.

"What is that?" Macey asked, letting the magic fall from her hands.

"I think it's one of the bookworms." Amber held it out.

The kelpie frowned, but didn't take it. The body was cut into segments, with a large round head and two antennae pointing out from it. The only thing Macey could compare it to was a caterpillar, though that wasn't quite right. The whole thing almost seemed like it was made out of parchment.

"What does it feel like?" she asked.

Amber cocked her head to the side, considering. "Kind of dry. A bit like paper, and if I squeeze, I'm worried it'll fall apart."

"Does the library not want that? I thought they were pests?" She hadn't seen any bookworms before.

Amber struggled to her feet, being careful not to use the hand with the worm in it. "Oh no, I don't think so. They don't eat books, they just absorb the knowledge." She carefully set the bookworm down on the shelf.

It looked at her with a surprisingly intent gaze and then disappeared into the books.

Amber leaned down and picked up the ones that had fallen to the floor.

"How did you fall over?" Macey asked.

The redhead flushed. "I tripped over my own feet," she admitted.

Macey snorted, but only because she knew they'd all done it at one point or another. Sometimes, it was impossible *not* to be clumsy.

"Do you need a hand?"

Amber shook her head. "I'm fine. I was bringing these back to the table anyway."

Despite her friend's insistence, Macey took some of the books from her to lighten the load. There was no need for her to struggle when Macey had two perfectly capable hands.

"Did you find what you needed?" she asked once the two of them were on the short walk back to the table they had saved.

"I don't know. But these are all ones that sound like they have the information I'm looking for."

"That's good. They really should put this on a database so we can access it any time we want," Macey muttered.

"You mean the Internet?" Amber joked. "We have that."

"It's not the same, though. It's harder to work out how much truth there is and..."

Amber laughed, cutting Macey off. "Because the authors of the ancient world are completely trustworthy? Don't you *remember* dealing with prophets?"

"Huh."

They arrived back at the table and set the books in a neat stack next to Amber's seat.

Satisfied that her friend was safe, Macey returned to her own. She picked up the egg and turned it over in her hand.

"Oh, no..."

"What is it?" Amber asked, peeking over the surprisingly large stack.

Macey gestured her over, unable to find the words to describe the horror over the small crack at the base of the egg.

"I'm so sorry, I must have cracked it when I came to help you." Guilt surged through her. She didn't want to have destroyed her friend's present.

"You can't have done," Amber protested. "It isn't

possible. Look." She flicked through the pages of the book Macey had been looking through and pointed to the first paragraph about eggs.

Macey read the words. "Tough shells, virtually impenetrable, protective..."

"See," Amber said, crossing her arms. "You can't have done anything to the egg, it isn't possible."

"Then what is it?" She ran a finger over the shell, trying to work out what the crack was.

The egg hissed and started to shake in her hands. The two women exchanged worried looks, neither of them having any idea what was happening.

Something slithered from the hole, wrapping itself around the hard shell of the egg. Its scales glinted in the light, the green a complete contrast to the golden shell. Macey had to admit that it was beautiful, even if it was terrifying.

"What is it?" Macey whispered.

"Why don't we ask it?" Amber suggested, looking as confused as the kelpie felt.

"It may have escaped your notice, but I don't speak serpent."

"Then it's a good job I do." Scales flickered over Amber's cheeks, but she didn't let a complete shift overtake her. She hissed out some words, though Macey couldn't tell what they meant. She'd never seen Amber do this before; it must have been a new skill she'd picked up.

The small snake wrapped around the egg made some noises in return.

"Well, what did it say?" Macey asked once Amber's face had returned to normal.

"It says it's an orphic egg." Amber cocked her head to the side and studied the egg intently.

"What does that mean?"

The beithir shrugged. "Who knows? But I guess we have something else to research while we're here."

"Do you have to sound so gleeful about that?" Macey muttered.

"Of course. Don't you miss saving the world? It's so fun!"

Macey rolled her eyes. Mostly because she agreed. She'd missed the rush of adrenaline and the excitement that came with discovering new dangers and challenges.

"Go on, look it up," the beithir encouraged.

"Why don't you do it?"

"Because you can't talk to the snake, silly. Hurry up."

Amber continued to do weird hissing noises. With a sigh, Macey got up and hurried to the reception desk. The kabouter was still sitting in the same position as earlier, looking at what seemed to be the same page of her dusty book.

"Excuse me, do you have anything on orphic eggs?" Macey asked breathlessly.

This time, the librarian looked up. Her sharp eyes were full of disdain as she took in Macey.

"Egg. Singular. There's only one orphic egg."

Macey sighed. "Yes, well, do you have anything on that orphic egg?"

The kabouter pursed her lips in disapproval and crossed her short arms in front of her chest. For someone resembling a large garden gnome, she looked very stern.

"I'm sorry, kaaba. I don't want to be rude, but it's really urgent."

The woman's eyebrows shot up when Macey used the honorific term for female elders.

"You speak our language?"

"That's one of the only Kabouter words I know," she admitted. "My boyfriend was raised by Kabouters."

The librarian's transformation couldn't have been more dramatic. A wide smile appeared on her face and her eyes sparkled with joy. She immediately seemed two decades younger, at the very least.

"Why didn't you say so, my dear. I'll show you the definite guide on the orphic egg. Or even better, I can give you a summary."

"Yes, please."

Macey grinned to herself as she followed the woman. She was glad she'd taken the time to learn some Kabouter etiquette when she'd last visited Jared's adopted family.

"According to Ancient Greek mythology, the very first god hatched from the orphic egg," the Kabouter explained while leading Macey through the maze of shelves. "Phanes, a hermaphroditic god, then created all the other Greek gods, including Zeus."

"And where did the egg come from?" Macey asked. She'd never heard of that myth, but then, she was more connected to Celtic mythology than Ancient Greek.

"It was created by Time itself, or Chronos. Of course, you have to take all those legends with a big pinch of salt. An entire salt grinder, to be honest. Some stories contradict each other, but what most of them agree on is that the egg had a snake wrapped around it, and that Phanes had both a phallus and a vagina. That's how he was able to create the other gods."

For a moment, Macey tried to imagine an ancient Greek god trying to have sex with himself, but then decided it wasn't worth her sanity.

"You were very particular about there being only one egg..." she began.

"Of course. There was only one creation. What use would a second egg be? Phanes created the gods, and together they shaped the world. If you believe the Ancient Greeks, anyway. After all, every culture has their own creation myth. What's fascinating though is that the egg myth reappears throughout the world. The Egyptians had the Cosmic Egg, from which the sun god Ra was born, and so did the ancient Hindus. They called it the Brahmanda. If you want, I can give you some books on the other occurrences of a world-egg."

"Thank you," Macey said politely and noncommittally. "All that means that the orphic egg starts creation, right? So if an orphic egg was to appear now, it would herald a new beginning?"

The Kabouter stopped in her tracks and stared at Macey with wide eyes. "Or the end of everything. History teaches us that the occurrence of something new very often brings the old to extinction. Old traditions die out when modern life takes over. Languages disappear. Culture fades until it's forgotten. No, my dear, you really wouldn't want a world-egg to appear. Ever."

Macey swallowed hard. She was glad now that the librarian had led her away from Amber and the egg, to the opposite side of the magic section. She really didn't want the Kabouter to see the egg and have a heart attack.

The woman continued walking until they reached a shelf even dustier than most of the others. She pulled out a leather-bound volume and carefully handed it to Macey.

"This book tells the story of the orphic egg from the very beginning all the way to the various gods Phanes created. It goes into quite a lot of detail about the...practicalities too. I recommend you skip chapter seven if you're of a sensitive nature."

With that, she shuffled off, leaving Macey speech-less. Sensitive nature? She was tempted to open chapter seven right away, but she was very aware that the clock was ticking. She had to get back to Amber.

She clutched the book to her chest and ran down the aisles as quietly as she could. She didn't want to have to explain to the librarian what her hurry was about. By the time she reached the row of shelves where she'd left Amber, she was out of breath. She'd not done enough saving-the-world recently; she was completely out of shape.

The beithir sat on the floor with the egg in her lap.

The snake was wound around her wrist, no longer attached to the egg.

"Amber," Macey called out as soon as she was in reach. "Don't touch the egg!"

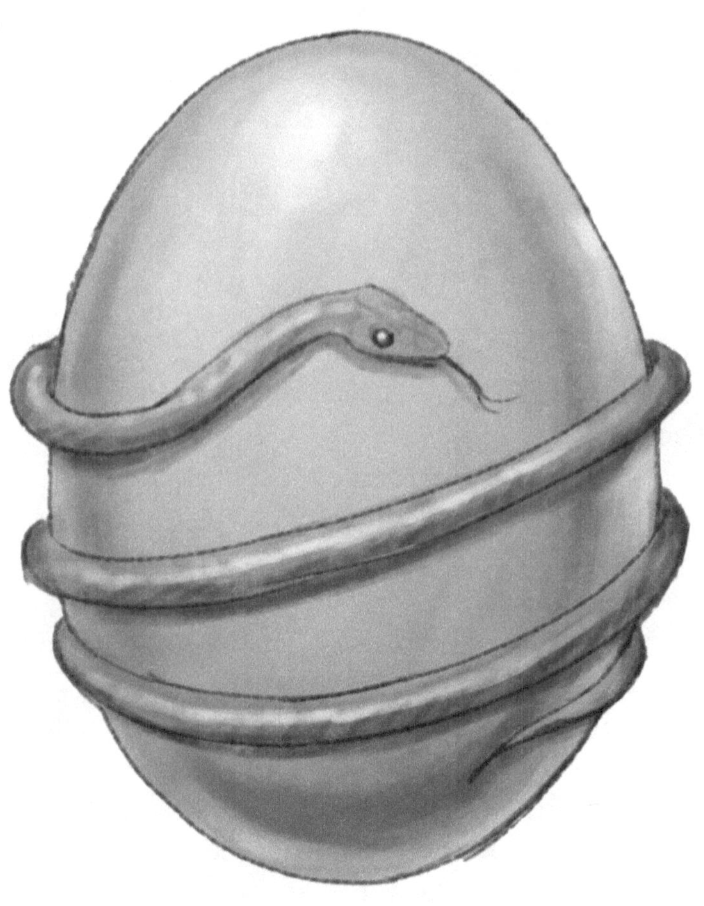

3

"You *took* a book from the British Library?" Izban asked, his eyes wide and serious. "You're not supposed to do that."

"It was special circumstances," Macey muttered.

"What the ice could be so special that it involved removing a priceless artefact from the most secure place on the planet?"

Macey snorted. "I wouldn't say the most secure place."

"Found him," Amber sang, walking through the kitchen door with Luc in tow. "What's going on here?" she asked, after looking between the two of them.

Macey hung her head. She hated putting Amber in this situation. She knew her best friend hated the tension that was always present between Macey and Izban.

"I'm in shock that the two of you thought this was a good idea," Izban said, clearly annoyed at Amber as well. That reassured Macey a little bit.

"It was special circumstances," the beithir reiterated, walking the rest of the way into the kitchen and hopping up onto one of the bar stools.

"So Macey said," Izban muttered.

"What are the circumstances?" Luc asked, following Amber over.

He kissed Macey on the cheek, before standing behind her and wrapping her tightly in his arms. She was vaguely aware of the small gusts of air which came from his wings. He didn't move them much while he was inside, but it was enough to cause small movements in the air.

"We made a friend," Amber announced, lifting up her arm and revealing the thin snake wrapped around it. The beithir's mood was even reflected in her tail, which flicked from side to side in excitement. Not for the first time, Macey found herself thinking of the way a dog's tail reacted when it was happy. Though from things the other woman had shared, Amber had a lot of control over it, and used her tails in ways that would make some people blush.

"Dare I ask what that is?" Izban asked.

Macey pointed to the golden egg still sat on the table, perfect save for the one hole where the snake had come out of.

Luc looked from the snake to the egg and sucked in a breath. This was why they'd looked for him as soon as they got back. He'd lived in Greece for a long time, if any of them had heard about the orphic egg, then it was going to be him. Izban had just happened to be in the kitchen when they'd returned.

"Is that what I think it is?" Luc asked.

"We think so. That's what we have the book for." Macey flashed Izban a pointed look.

"It shouldn't exist," Luc whispered. "How did you even get hold of it?"

"Izban got it for Amber thinking it was a dragon egg," she explained.

The mage at least seemed a little ashamed. "That's what the dealer said it was."

"And you didn't think to check?" Macey asked. "That seems a little short sighted after what we've all been through."

"I didn't want to go through the book to check. I assumed it would be fine," Izban protested.

Amber laughed. "You know what they say!"

When no one said anything, she tutted and sighed.

"You shouldn't assume, it makes an *ass* out of *u* and *me*." Her laughter was infectious, and despite the situation, Macey smiled.

"So, what do you know about it?" she asked Luc.

"That it isn't good news."

Macey rolled her eyes. "I got that much. Why do we never end up taking care of something cute like the Easter Bunny?"

Izban snorted. "You think he's cute? He's a sadist. Never happy."

Macey ignored the comment, not wanting to ruin her image of a cute rabbit delivering chocolate eggs to the children of the world.

"Do you know how to stop it from opening?" she asked Luc.

Amber tickled the tiny snake's head and cooed to it. Apparently her friend had gotten the pet she wanted, even if it wasn't a dragon. For the first time, Macey hoped she wouldn't have to destroy the bad thing in order to save the world. Amber was bonding with it.

"There is no stopping it. The egg is linked to creation. That just kind of...happens." Luc shrugged,

She leaned back into him, taking comfort from him, even if he didn't have the answers. "Hmm." Macey wasn't too happy about that option. Anything that stopped the world turning the way it should be wasn't good in her opinion.

"Will any of the others know how to deal with it?" Izban asked.

Macey pursed her lips. Luc was the most well versed in mythology from his part of the world, but the others had been around a long time too, which meant they knew things that could be useful.

"It's worth asking them," Luc said. "And what about the book?"

"I haven't had a chance to read it yet," Macey admitted. "I thought it was best to find out what we knew first, and then go from there."

"You didn't want to read, did you?" he teased.

Macey twisted around in his arms and looked up at him sternly. "I would never skip on my reading. But when saving the world is concerned, I've learned that time is of the essence."

"Ah, yes, but so is knowledge." He leaned in and kissed her on the nose.

Izban made a gagging sound behind her, but Macey didn't turn to look.

"Oh quit moaning," Amber said. "We're as bad as they are."

"They only have to watch it once, though. We have to watch it four more times," he muttered.

"Then if you really want to get even, I'll simply go find four more guys. Should be fairly simple. I think there was another beithir back home who..."

Izban growled, and Macey was certain the two of them would be kissing in moments. For some reason, Amber teasing him about his jealousy got him riled up.

"Come on, let's leave them to it and go find the others," Luc suggested. "We can't fit all eight of us in the room at once anyway."

"That's true. Though the house would probably make the room bigger," Macey pointed out.

"Or you could humour me, and let me have a moment alone with you," he suggested instead.

"Perhaps." She smirked and unwrapped herself from him. She took Luc's hand and pulled him from the room, leaving the couple alone in the kitchen.

"Macey," he said as soon as they were out of earshot. "Wait a second before we look for the others."

Immediately, the corridor became longer and darker, as if the house wanted to make sure that they had a moment of privacy.

"Thank you, house," she whispered, as always a little self-conscious of talking to a building.

"I didn't want to say this in front of Amber," Luc

began. His brows were drawn together with worry. "But I think we have a problem."

"Besides some kind of creation event happening in an already existing world?"

He didn't smile. "I think the snake thinks Amber is her mother."

Macey's mouth dropped open. "Say what?"

"You know the riddle, what came first, the chicken or the egg?"

"Of course, we even have that in our loch, although our version is whether the fish or the spawn came first."

"In Greek mythology, the first god was born from the orphic egg, but the egg didn't just pop into existence. It was *made*. In effect, that means the egg has parents. Or the god inside, depending on how you look at it. Now, the first thing the snake saw after hatching was you and Amber. Which would make both of you its parents, except that Amber spoke to it in its own language. A bond was formed, unintentionally or not."

"What does that mean?"

Luc sighed. "I don't know. If we're lucky, Amber will have full authority over the snake and whatever it guards. If not, then Amber could be in danger."

"As well as the world," Macey muttered darkly. "How did we even get here? This was supposed to be a fun trip to the library, and now we're having to save the world once again."

The daimon's lips twitched. "You attract trouble like a beautiful magnet, my little kelpie."

He opened his arms and she stepped into his hug. He nuzzled her hair while folding his wings around her. She loved when he did that. It made her feel safe and loved.

"We'll figure it out," he whispered. "We've faced impossible tasks before."

Macey nodded. They had indeed. And they'd been successful every single time, although the cost had been high in some cases. She forced herself not to think of the people who died in the fight against the Mahoun. It was too painful. Macey and the Wardens were all still alive, but not everyone was.

"Does this mean that Izban will be the snake's dad?" she asked, the thought suddenly popping into her head.

Luc snorted. "Only you could come up with a question like that."

"Will he though?"

"I have no idea. But let's not assume that the snake will stay around. There's little mention in mythology of what becomes of the snake after the egg opens for good. It may just be a temporary guardian and then disappear."

Macey could already imagine how disappointed Amber would be if her new pet disappeared. Maybe they'd be able to make it stay, although only if the cost of it wasn't the safety of the entire world. She loved Amber, but not enough to risk billions of lives for her. She wouldn't do that for her men, either. It would break her, but she'd learned a lot in the past year, like seeing the bigger picture.

Luc pressed a kiss on her forehead and stepped back, unwrapping his beautiful wings. "Let's find the others."

To Macey's frustration, none of the guys were surprised that she'd managed to get herself in trouble. Even though she kept telling them that the whole dragon egg thing hadn't been her idea.

"What if it's a good god inside the egg?" Jared asked over the noise of everyone talking. "It could be a god of love."

He licked his lips suggestively and grinned.

"There are no gods," Macey said automatically, but her words sounded hollow.

"Maybe, maybe not," Cam replied, looking the most serious of everyone, with the exception of Luc. "But that doesn't mean some very powerful being or magic is lurking within the egg. Is there some way we can destroy it before it fully hatches?"

Flint's eyes widened slightly. "You want to destroy it? But then we'll never know what was inside."

"And that's a good thing," Cam snapped. "I don't know about you, but I rather like the world as it is. Yes, there's a lot of bad stuff happening, but at least it's not the apocalypse. If the egg is gone, we can just continue with our lives as before."

"I doubt we could break it," Luc said, and the room went quiet. He always had that effect. "It may look like an oversized chicken egg, but it's something much more than that. No, we need more information before we can make a proper plan of what to do."

Macey nodded. "I agree. First, I think we should ask the snake. Well, Amber should, since she's the only one able to communicate with it. The snake already told her that it's an orphic egg, so maybe it'll be prepared to divulge more secrets. But we also need to find out where Izban got it from. That might give us a clue to what's inside or why someone would even sell it."

Luc gave her a proud smile. It could have felt patronising, but he was her daimon, her guardian and guide, and she was aware of how much older and wise he was. Most of the time, anyway.

"I shall look into some of the older texts on orphic eggs. Who wants to help me?"

Ronan lifted his hand. He'd stayed quiet so far, but his eyes shone with enthusiasm for the task. "I think I've read something about a world-egg in selkie traditions. Maybe there's a connection. I'll look it up, then I'll come join you, Luc." He looked at Macey. "And we'll reschedule our date."

Of course. It was her and Ronan's date night. She had one a week with each guy, to give them the chance to spend time with just each other. Before they'd introduced that schedule, she'd constantly felt guilty about not spending equal time with each of her five men, even though she knew that was technically impossible. They all lived together, and most nights they shared one giant bed, but they all had different interests and responsibilities. None of them had jobs per se, but Jared spent a lot of time helping his Kabouter family, Luc was involved in daimon politics, Ronan was trying to mend his relationship with his selkies, Cam had started learning more about seelies, while Flint had taken up cooking. With not much success.

"Of course we'll reschedule," Macey said with a smile. "Waffles in Bruges?"

He nodded. "Waffles it is."

Now she had an extra incentive to deal with their egg problem quickly. She'd not had waffles in at least three days. Maybe even four. What a travesty. If it had been up to her, waffles would have been on the menu every single day.

"Cam and I will talk with Izban and accompany him to wherever he got the egg from," Flint volunteered.

That left just Jared. "I'll come with you. Maybe I can seduce the snake into behaving."

Cam laughed. "You just want to have first dibs on the god of love."

"There are no gods," Macey sighed. One day, she'd be able to prove that. Until then, she just had to repeat it again and again, even when confronted with a giant egg that was supposed to birth the god of creation.

4

"The snake wants to talk to you," Amber announced the moment Macey walked back into the kitchen to pick up the book she'd brought from the library. There was no point in them bringing it to the house in the mists if they weren't going to look at what it said.

"Through you?"

Amber nodded and then turned back to the snake and tickled it under the chin. "Isn't it the cutest?"

"Sure," Macey agreed, not feeling it as much as Amber clearly was.

"This is so much better than a dragon."

"Amber, you know that thing could destroy the world, right?" Macey asked. She was used to her friend being the most upbeat of all of them, but this was different. Something about the way she was talking to and touching the snake was off.

"Yes, but it doesn't want to," she assured her, giving the snake some more gooey eyes.

Macey sighed quietly, not wanting to frustrate her

friend any more than she had to, though she was concerned about the situation. The more attached Amber got to the snake, the harder things would be if they had to kill it.

"What did the snake want to tell me?" Macey asked, knowing there was nothing else she could say.

"I don't know. It said you should touch the egg with both hands and it would be able to communicate with you." The redhead didn't even look at her as she spoke. It was sweet in a way, but rather concerning in another.

"If something happens to me, tell the others where I am," Macey said. She'd learned that the best thing she could do was go with the flow and see what happened. Perhaps the others believed more in researching and facing things with more knowledge, but it always ended up boring her. She was more of a hands-on person.

She snorted. In this case she really would be hands-on with the egg.

She rolled up her sleeves and made her way over to the golden shell. She'd better get waffles after this. If not, then it really wasn't worth it.

Macey took a deep breath and placed both of her hands on the egg.

"What's supposed..." Her question was cut off by a fuzzy feeling running up and down her entire body. That wasn't a good sign.

Everything spun out of control, then turned black. Macey opened and closed her eyes, trying to work out where she was and what was happening. She'd been in the kitchen before, touching the egg.

Oh no. Was she *inside* the egg? How was that possible?

She shook her head. She needed to get with the program on that front. She'd found herself in impossible situations before, and had always managed to get out of them. This would simply be the latest in a long line of crazy stories she'd have about her life. One thing was for certain, when she *did* have kids, she'd have some great stories to tell them.

"Hello?" she called out. "You wanted to talk to me?"

"Hello, Macey," a male voice responded, the hint of a hiss in his voice. Was it the snake wrapped around Amber's wrist, or was it something else?

"How do you know my name?" she asked the man. No. Not man. God.

"Amber told us."

"Us?" That didn't sound good.

"Yes. Us. The god, the snake, and the egg. At the moment, we are one being and three."

"Only at the moment?" Macey asked.

"Things will change in time," the god said. "I'm not meant to live in an egg forever."

"So you and the snake are separate things?" She didn't miss the hint of hope in her own voice. Perhaps Amber would be able to keep the small reptile after all.

"Yes and no. At the moment, we are the same. Once I am released, we are not. The snake isn't to be blamed for this. It has no will but mine at this moment in time."

Dread sank in the pit of Macey's stomach as she considered what he might mean. Was this god good or bad? And what about the egg itself?

"How did you come into being?" she asked the god.

"How did you?" he returned.

This would be a lot easier if she could see the god's face while he talked, but the inside of the egg was pitch black. Perhaps the god had no form yet. She supposed that would make sense.

Creation normally came from darkness no matter which culture it seemed to belong to.

"What are your intentions?" she asked with her head held high. She had become quite good at talking to baddies.

"At the moment, they are threefold. The egg does not want to be destroyed. The snake wants to stay with its new friend. And the god..."

"Yes?"

"The god has a task to fulfil. His own intentions don't matter."

Macey made a mental note to come back to that. It sounded like the god wasn't happy about not having a choice about having to follow orders.

"And what is that task?"

"We are not sure if we should tell you."

She sighed. "You told Amber you wanted to speak to me. I'm here now, so go and talk. What's your purpose? And how can I help?"

"You want to help?" The god sounded surprised.

"It's what I do. And I'm actually pretty good at it. I've saved the world more than once." She tried to hide her pride from her voice, but failed. Not that she had to blame herself for being self-confident. She was only telling the truth.

"You have."

It was not a question. Macey was beginning to ask herself how much this god knew of the outside world. Was he omnipotent? Or had he been sleeping in this egg for all his life with no way of knowing what was going on outside?

"Do you have a name?" she asked.

"We are the orphic egg."

"Yes, I know that. I mean, does the god have a name?"

"He does. I do."

This conversation was getting more and more confusing. It felt like she was talking to one, male person slash god, but apparently that wasn't true. She found it hard to believe though that the egg was also speaking to her as part of the trinity consciousness.

"And would you like to tell me that name?"

"Once my name is spoken, the shell will break and I will enter the mortal world. Do you want me to do that?"

Macey wrung her hands in frustration. "How am I supposed to know? If you're a good god, someone who will bring peace, health, prosperity, stuff like that, then yes, go ahead. if you're a god of war, illness and destruction, then no, I want you to stay inside this egg for all eternity."

She stopped, realising she was talking as if she believed in gods. When had that happened? This could all be a trick. Some kind of powerful entity pretending to be a god. Gods weren't real. Right? It was sounding more and more hollow in her mind.

"As I said, the god's intentions aren't his own. There is a task to fulfil, a price to pay and a reward to reap."

"Great. Yet more mysteries. Can't you just go back to sleep and be done with it?"

To her surprise, the voice laughed. "We wish, my child. Now that we awake, we will have to find our guardians who will help us fulfil our destiny."

"Guardians?"

A feeling of dread bloomed in Macey's stomach.

"Yes. Seven guardians are prophesied to come to our aid. They will shield us from danger while we carry out our task."

"Ehm... does your prophecy definitely say seven?"

"I would not joke about something as important."

"No, of course you wouldn't." Macey sighed. "Let's say I knew the guardians you needed. What happens after you're done with your task?"

"Then I shall go and rest with my forefathers."

That sounded good. Now she just had to find out what that task was. Sadly, it was easier to pull the teeth out of a sleeping ceasg's maw than getting answers from this guy.

"If I promise to show you the way to the guardians, can you tell me what you intend? Please?"

The god stayed silent for a while. Macey twiddled her thumbs, expecting nothing good to come out of this.

"Agreed," he said finally. "But if you do not deliver me to the seven guardians, I shall have to kill you."

"Deal."

A tingle ran over her skin; the feeling of magic.

He'd done something to her, probably to make sure she couldn't break her promise.

"My task is to bring new life to the world."

Relief flooded over Macey. Life was good. Really good. It wasn't war or famine or other horrible things.

"New life for the guardians," the god continued. "My task is to make sure that two children are born to the guardians. Two unrelated children, so that they may create the new generation of guardians that the world will need in future. A new prophecy will come to pass, a new danger lurking in the darkness. These children are essential for life to continue."

Macey was speechless. Had he just said that she needed to become pregnant?

"What's your name?" she asked breathlessly, barely hanging on to sanity.

"The god's name is Eros."

5

Pain pounded through Macey's head, and it took her a moment to realise that meant she was outside the egg again. Bracing herself for the effect the light would have on her eyes, she looked up to find Amber still fussing the snake on her arm.

"How long was I gone?" she asked, surprised to find there was no croak in her voice. For some reason, she'd expected one, and it was odd for it not to happen.

"Gone? You've been here the whole time. I thought you were waiting for the egg to do something." Amber nodded to the golden shell, which still lay under Macey's hands.

"Oh." She pulled away from it and sat back. "How long since I touched it?"

Amber shrugged. "A couple of minutes. If that. Have you been gone longer?"

This was one of the many things she liked about having a best friend who'd gone through the same things she had. When she implied that weird things had happened, Amber would believe her without a second thought. It was reassuring.

"It feels like it. But you know how these things are."

Amber nodded sagely. "What did the snake say to you?"

"It wasn't the snake," Macey corrected quickly. "I talked to the god." The sentence sounded weird, even though she'd just talked to him. She'd spent so long under the impression that gods didn't exist, and yet here one was. Then again, she supposed that if someone had told her three years ago that beithirs were real, then she wouldn't have believed them either, and yet here she was being best friends with one of the flying reptiles.

"Well, that changes everything. Was it a good god, or a bad one?" Amber asked, pulling her attention away from the snake for the first time since they'd returned.

Macey grimaced. "That depends, how ready are you for children?"

A horrified look crossed the other woman's face. "Considering I'm barely twenty, I'll pass. Do you have any idea how old beithirs normally are when they start having kids?"

Macey raised an eyebrow. "Surprisingly, my knowledge of the beithir reproductive system is limited," she deadpanned.

"I doubt I even *can* get pregnant yet," Amber said.

"Wait, what?"

"Most beithirs have children around a hundred. I'm nowhere close to that. I've never heard of a beithir my age having a child. Why?"

"The god said it needed the seven guardians to have two unrelated children so there would be guardians for the next generation..."

"Not until the ice caps melt," Izban seethes from the door.

Amber shot him a stern look. "We're having kids one day," she pointed out.

"Of course we are," he said quickly, covering up his slip.

The beithir didn't look pacified, which caused Macey to have to smother a laugh. Seeing Izban uncomfortable was always fun to her, even if it shouldn't be.

"Well? Are you going to explain?" Amber tapped her foot on the ground.

Perhaps it would be best if Macey left the room, though she didn't want to miss whatever this was, especially as Izban might have a solution. He was one of the most well versed of them all when it came to obscure magic, and they might be in need of that.

"I don't want my child to be a Warden. It's not a life for anyone. You can't say either of you would choose it for yourselves." He looked between the two women.

"No," Macey admitted. "I want to keep any children I have far away from the things we had to deal with." She'd thought about it a couple of times, and always come to the conclusion that she'd do anything possible to protect her offspring.

"Then what do we do?" Amber asked.

"The god seemed pretty adamant about what he expected," Macey mused. "But I think we should have this conversation away from the egg." She gave a pointed look to the snake wound around Amber's arm too. Whether the beithir liked it or not, the snake was *part* of the orphic egg, and if it was still linked to the god, then it could hear everything they said.

Amber gave the creature a longing look, but seemed to understand what she had to do. Scales flickered across her face, and then she hissed.

The snake reared its head and bared its fangs. Despite the amount of times she found herself disagreeing with him, Macey shared a worried look with Izban. They had no way of knowing what would happen if the snake bit Amber. In theory, she was immune to snake venom, but this was a mythical egg that was supposedly responsible for all of creation. That didn't sound like it would obey the normal laws of poisoning.

Amber held her free hand up to stop either of them taking action.

It took another moment for the snake to respond and loosen its coils from around Amber's wrist. Macey breathed a sigh of relief as it slithered onto the table and back towards the golden shell of the egg. It wound itself back in position, looking as much at home as it had on Amber's wrist.

That was a good thing. It had to be.

"Right, let's go sort this out." Amber slipped her hand into Izban's and began to pull him out of the kitchen. "Wait, where are the others?" she asked Macey.

The kelpie shook her head. "Third door on the left."

Amber almost skipped down the corridor, causing Izban to do a weird shuffle.

"Do you know anything that might help with the situation?" she asked the mage as she fell into step beside him.

"I'm not sure." Something in his voice told her he was thinking things through. "Though there might be something in an old fertility ritual I read about..."

"I thought we decided we were doing this without babies?" Amber said, looking back at the two of them.

"I hope," Macey muttered, though she had to admit the image of her men with a baby to dote on was appealing. They weren't ready yet, though. She was still getting used to splitting her time between the kelpies in the loch who called her Queen, and the ones in the sea that called her an Empress. Even with her Mother and cousin to help, there was still a lot for Macey to get her head around.

Amber pushed open the door.

Four sets of eyes swung around to meet them.

"Where's Ronan?" Macey asked.

"He went for a swim," Flint answered, setting down the book he was searching through and shuffling over so she could sit next to him.

"Not the best time for that," Izban said offhandedly.

"He said it would help him think better," Jared put in. "And I don't blame him. Certain things help me think clearer too, though it's better if I'm not alone." He winked at Macey.

She giggled despite herself. She should be used to the way he made her feel by now, but the incubus still had the same effect as when they first met. It was odd how much and how little things had changed.

"We've not found much," Luc admitted. "Just that it's bad news."

"Macey might have some more news for you there," Amber chirped in.

"Where's the snake?" Luc asked, glancing down at her bare wrist.

"In the kitchen with the egg."

Cam was on his feet in seconds. "Should we really be leaving that thing alone?"

"It's fine," Amber assured him. "The snake is watching the egg, nothing is going to happen to it."

"You don't know that..."

"But I do," Macey put in before they could deteriorate into a full-blown argument. It had happened before, and no doubt it would happen again. The eight of them spent too much time around one another for it to never blow up. "The god told me what he wanted." She launched into an explanation of what had happened in the egg.

Thankfully, Ronan walked in just as she was starting, so she wouldn't have to repeat this all to him once she'd finished.

Luc looked between the two women. "But Amber isn't old enough to have children yet."

"Yes, that's one of the problems we have," Macey acknowledged. "The other one being that I doubt any of us want our children to have to become like us."

Silence met her statement.

"Perhaps it's almost inevitable," Flint said. "We're all powerful..."

"Wardenship doesn't run in the family," Izban countered.

"It has done," Luc said, glancing at Macey as he said it.

"All the other Wardens have been humans." Izban ran a hand through his shocking blue hair. "Haven't they?"

"That's what we were told," Flint said.

"But that doesn't take into account that my father was a Warden," Macey said.

More silence followed as the information sank in. She wasn't sure how it had worked. In theory, a kelpie-human baby should have been *less* powerful, not more. And yet, that hadn't been the case. Of course, some of that was probably because she was the Water Warden herself.

"Is there any way we can give it what it wants without having to endanger our future children?" Jared asked. "I'm with Macey, I don't want our child exposed to that. Never mind that we won't even know whose powers they've inherited until after."

She didn't say it aloud, but it also left her relationships with Luc and Ronan in a precarious situation unless she knew the exact moment when she conceived. Emotionally, they were strong enough to weather it, she was certain of it, but she didn't *want* to give up the physical side of their relationship.

Don't worry, little kelpie, it won't come to that, Luc's voice came through her head.

I thought I told you not to do that, she scolded. They'd been practicing mental communication lately in case they needed it.

I didn't think you'd want me to say that aloud and reveal your thoughts.

You shouldn't have been listening to them anyway, she scolded, though her heart wasn't in it. This wasn't the worst voice she'd ever had in her head.

"There's something we can try," Izban said. "But I need to do some reading on it first, and we'll need to go to the place where one of us was born..." he looked around the room.

"Cam and I don't remember our childhood," Flint said with a shrug.

"Different realm," Luc added.

"I was born in the middle of a lightning storm," Amber said brightly.

They turned to look at Macey. She sighed. "I guess it's time to go see Nessie."

6

Nessie was enjoying her retirement. She was stretched out on a lounge chair by the beach, surrounded by three young, very fit guys with abs that would have made Macey drool if she had been single. They'd found her in the Bahamas, where Nessie had bought herself a villa with sea views. Now that the world was safe and the kelpie kingdom in safe hands, Macey's mother had decided to live the good life.

One of the young men hurried off to get them some drinks, while another continued fanning Nessie with a plastic palm leaf. Macey rolled her eyes. She'd always thought Nessie to be one of the most down-to-the-loch-floor kelpies, but it seemed that with age that was changing. Not that she had any idea how old Nessie really was. Her mother refused to talk about that subject, preferring to keep up the mystery.

Nessie pushed up her sunglasses and smiled at Macey and the other Wardens.

"Hey, sweetie."

Macey cringed. "You've never called me sweetie before."

"Then you better get used to it." Nessie grinned at the young man next to her. His only job seemed to be posing as the dedicated eye candy. "This gentleman loves it when I call him sweetie, right?"

He nodded indulgently.

Macey couldn't help but roll her eyes. "Nessie, we need to talk. Alone."

"She doesn't like calling me mum in front of other people," the older kelpie stage-whispered. "But in private she's very affectionate."

What the waves was wrong with Nessie? It had to be the sun. Heatstroke. After all, they were from Scotland and not used to sunbathing. Macey better get her mother out of the sun before the kelpie's brain fried completely.

"How about we go inside," Macey suggested with a certain forcefulness. "I feel my scales melting in this heat."

Nessie sighed dramatically. "You're so impatient. But alright then, only because I have the most delicious mango liqueur waiting for us in the fridge."

"How many of those have you had today?" Amber asked innocently, shooting Macey an exasperated look.

"Just a tipple or two. Right, Bastian?"

Nessie looked at eye candy for reassurance.

"Yes, just a few," he said with a grin. "Shall I help you inside?"

He held out an arm and Nessie took it, letting him pull her up from the lounger. The Nessie of old would have never behaved like that, Macey thought. She'd been a strong and fiercely independent kelpie who would have bitten off the hand of whoever offered to help her with something. She hoped it was just age and not something more serious.

Macey breathed a sigh of relief once they were inside the cool villa. The living room was looking out towards the sea, giving the most amazing view, and the beach style furniture helped with the impression that they were still outside. Luckily, it was a much better temperature in there.

The young man who'd left when they'd arrived returned with a tray of cocktails. Once they'd all taken a glass, Nessie waved him and the other two guys away. Finally.

"We have a bit of a problem," Macey began.

"Haven't you always," Nessie interrupted with a good-natured smile. "What is it this time? Saving the world again?"

"Preventing us from getting pregnant," Macey blurted. "And then saving the world, yes."

She gave her mother a quick summary of what had been going on.

Nessie's eyes widened when she revealed the god's name. "Eros? The god of love? The Greek equivalent of Cupid?"

"The very same. And I never saw him, so who knows if he has a bow and arrows, ready to shoot me."

"Do you think his arrows could impregnate us?" Amber asked with a worried frown. "He might be able to cause an immaculate conception."

Izban snorted. "You're not immaculate anymore, snakey." He cleared his throat. "Ehm...Amber."

Macey couldn't help but grin despite the seriousness of the situation. Izban was right, there definitely weren't any virgins in this room. And she knew that if she really had to get pregnant, her guys would gladly do the deed themselves rather than let Eros interfere.

"Anyway, we may have a plan," Macey continued. "But for that, we need to go to the place where I was born. I assume it was in the loch, but I need to know where exactly. In the Palace somewhere?"

Nessie looked increasingly uncomfortable. "No, not in the palace."

"Then where in the loch?"

"Not in the loch."

"Nessie, just tell me, this is important." Macey felt a little sorry for being so impatient, but the worry of her potentially having to have a child was weighing heavy on her.

"You can't go there," Nessie said without meeting her daughter's eyes. "You will have to find someone else's birthplace."

"None of us have one that we can go to," Jared explained. "I don't know where I was born; I was raised by Kabouters but I wasn't born in their caves. Macey is the only one."

The older kelpie finally looked up. "You were born between realities, Macey. I birthed you in the room where the dead Wardens used to wait for the next generation, so that your father could witness the birth. But that room no longer exists. You said so yourself. I myself wasn't able to travel there anymore after your birth; that day was the final time I saw your father. It was both the happiest and the saddest day of my life."

Macey stared at her mother. She hadn't known. She always thought her father - her real father, not her adoptive dad - had never seen her, and that she'd never seen him, but that wasn't true. In the first moments of her life, she had to have seen her father. Not that she'd ever be able to remember, but the thought filled her heart with warmth.

"We definitely can't go there," Luc said solemnly. "Nessie is right, that Warden room no longer exists, since you're the last generation of Wardens."

"Except that we're not," Amber replied with excitement. "Eros said as much. If our children-"

"Hypothetical children," Izban interrupted.

"-hypothetical children are going to be Wardens as well, the room might have reopened."

Luc shook his head. "No, it's gone."

Macey didn't ask how he knew that. Luc's daimon magic was special and often gave him knowledge that even he himself didn't understand.

Suddenly, one of the shirtless guys ran into the room.

"Ma'am, there's someone outside!"

"That's not exactly something special, this isn't a private beach," Nessie began but then turned to look out of the window, as did everyone else.

Macey sucked in a breath. A man stood outside, staring at the house. There was no doubt about who he was.

His golden skin shimmered in the sunshine, but she bet it would also glow in the midst of night. His sleek hair curled down to his shoulders, the same colour as his golden wings. They were shorter than Luc's black wings, but no less impressive. What stood out the most, however, was that he was naked and...

"Don't look," Nessie said with a gasp. "You don't need to see that."

Jared laughed. "Don't worry, she's seen bigger."

As much as she loved Jared's cock, there was no doubt that Eros - no doubt it was him - had a much bigger dick. And he was fully erect. Did the god always walk around like that or was he especially excited to see Macey and the others?

On his hip hung a quiver filled with silver arrows, while a bow was casually swung around his back. He cut an impressive figure - and a scary one.

"I assume that's Eros?" Amber squeaked before clearing her throat. "You didn't say he looked that hot."

"I didn't see him in the egg. And besides, he's not that hot. More like oversized and oversexed."

Izban nodded. "Definitely. He's just showing off."

Slowly, the god readied his bow and pointed it right at Macey.

"Hey, we had a deal!" she shouted, but she wasn't sure he'd be able to hear her through the closed window. He didn't respond, didn't acknowledge her words at all. Instead, he pulled the bowstring and let an arrow fly. It didn't hit the window as Macey'd hoped, but passed through it, as if the glass wasn't there at all.

Just before the arrow pierced Macey's heart, Nessie jumped in front of her daughter.

Nessie crumpled to the ground, causing Macey to cry out. She dropped to her knees next to the prone body of her mother, cradling her. Just as she was about to start begging the older kelpie to wake up, her eyes cracked open.

"Well, I can safely say that's never happened before," Nessie said.

"What..." Macey started, unsure what question she even wanted to ask.

"Eros' arrow," Izban explained. "He hit her with it, and now..." She sensed the discomfort coming from him in waves.

"Now I'm going to make the most of this gift." Nessie gestured for the man still standing outside, and Macey had no doubt what she intended to do to him. Nor that she wanted to be here when her mother started to *do* said things. "Stay safe, daughter."

Macey rose to her feet. "Are you going to be okay?"

"Oh, I'll be more than okay, don't worry about me," her mother said, a wide grin on her face.

"Please..."

"Stay safe, yes, I know," Nessie reiterated. "You should visit when you're done saving the world. Particularly if you're planning on giving me a grandchild. Though the waves know I'm too young to be a Granny."

Macey cracked a smile at that. "I'm too young to be a mother, too. I don't think I'd do a good job."

Nessie's eyes softened. "You'd make an amazing mother, no matter how old you are. But if you're not ready, don't let anything as simple as a god force the issue."

"I'll try not to. But I don't know how to stop it." She glanced over her shoulder to check what Eros was doing, but he was standing completely still, almost as if he was recharging.

"Oh, my sweet child. Since when have you let something as simple as not knowing the answer stop you from saving the world? We both know you're capable of great things."

"I hope you're right."

"I am. You're one of the most resourceful people in the world. And you have the strength of the other Wardens and your consorts to pull on. You may have fulfilled the original prophecy, but that doesn't mean anything. You can make anything happen if you put your mind to it," Nessie said. "Now, go deal with a god. And remember, they're only slightly more powerful than you. I'm going to make the most of being struck by a certain someone's arrow." She leaned in and kissed Macey on the cheek, before walking back to her hut, the men in tow.

Macey shook her head. The older kelpie certainly didn't *act* her age. But perhaps that was a good thing. It kept her busy and out of harm's way.

"She's right, you know," Luc said. "The gods aren't exactly what they claim to be."

"Should we maybe not have this conversation in front of him," Jared muttered. "I can feel him watching, and it makes me *very* uncomfortable."

"Aren't you a sex being?" Izban asked. "You should be bowing at his feet..."

"And would you do the same if a certain snow queen appeared and demanded something from you?" Jared threw back.

Macey smothered a laugh. Jared had begged her to keep his love of animated musicals to herself, and here he was outing it the first chance he got.

The blank look Izban flashed him was enough to convince Macey that the reference was lost on him.

"What he's saying is that he doesn't have an automatic affinity to him," Macey put in. Then she turned to the others and beckoned them into a huddle. "Where do we think he won't follow us?" she asked.

Ronan looked at the god, who was still standing as still as before. "Do you think he can breathe underwater?"

Macey sighed. "Only one way to find out. But where is it best for us to go? St. Kilda has all your people on it..."

The selkie shuddered. "Best not there. What about the loch?"

"And we still don't know where any of us were born," Cam said. "Which means that we probably can't satisfy the god the way he wants to be."

"Stop talking about him when he's standing right there," Macey instructed. "He might be able to hear us anywhere we go..."

"Except a void," Amber suggested. "Or the echo of one." A knowing smile spread over her face.

"Is it me, or is she looking more devious than normal?" Flint asked.

"Which one do you think we should try?" Luc asked.

Macey thought through the voids they'd closed, wondering which one of them would be their best, and safest, choice given the circumstances.

"Wouldn't it be fitting if we went to the city of love?" she suggested, shooting another look at the god.

Luc chuckled. "Paris, here we come."

7

Macey stepped out of the Staran and into the catacombs beneath Paris. Unlike the last time they'd been here, the whole place was silent, and the piles of bones didn't move at all. That was a relief, she didn't think she could cope with fighting any gashadokuro this time. One god was enough.

"Does anyone remember exactly where the void is?" she asked.

"Yes," Cam answered, and pushed through the small crowd. He led them through the twisted tunnels with ease.

"Will someone make a light before I trip over my own feet?" Izban grumbled.

Flint clicked his fingers, and a couple of balls of flame flickered into life above the Wardens.

They continued walking, the only sounds around them were the clicking of their feet along the floor.

"Where have the lampads gone?" Macey asked after a while. The last time they'd been here, one of the flame people had taken them to where the void had been ripping away their magic, but she didn't sense any of them around right now.

Flint shrugged. "I don't sense anything with fire magic nearby. Maybe they've moved on and found somewhere else to make their nest? If the voids have left an imprint on the world, then it couldn't have been comfortable for them."

"We're here," Cam announced before Macey could respond.

The eight of them fanned out and stared at the black space in front of them. A couple of years ago, the sight would have filled Macey with dread, as it would have meant they'd had to face one of the Mahoun's siblings and save the French lampads. But this time, it was only because of the emptiness around them and nothing more sinister.

"Are we sure we're safe here?" Macey asked.

Amber shrugged. "It's just a theory. But can't you feel the lack of magic in the air?"

Macey reached out to pull magic into herself, and found the beithir was right. She let the connection to the power around her vanish, lest she use it up and leave Flint with none to control the fireballs above them.

"So, what are we going to do about the god?" Macey asked, looking between each of their faces.

Luc's wings flapped, pulling her attention to him. "I've heard rumours that the gods aren't as powerful as they tried to make humans believe at the start. It's why there haven't been any new ones for a long time."

"Wait, so that *thing* isn't all powerful?" Amber asked.

The daimon shrugged. "There's no real way of knowing if it's true. But there's a chance that it isn't."

"If it isn't all powerful, then it can't have the power to destroy the world," Cam said.

"No," Flint agreed. "And we can trap it in some way. But how?"

"We give it what it wants," Macey said, understanding of how they were going to get through this washing over her in a moment. It relied on everything they thought they knew being true, and a couple of other things, but she was almost certain they could manage it.

All seven of them turned to her, confusion on their faces.

"You heard the bit about me not being able to have children, right?" Amber checked.

Macey nodded. "But clearly *Eros* doesn't know that. So we agree to what he wants, then lull him into a less alert state, then we can trap him in some kind of container or jar." She looked at Luc, hoping he'd confirm that was possible.

He grinned. "What do you think Pandora's box really was."

"All right. Then here's what we do." She took a deep breath, knowing this could go *very* wrong for them. "We're going to go back to the house and summon the god. Then we're going to tell him we've agreed to his demands. We'll do everything we can *not* to fulfil them, but go through the motions, so to speak. Because he wants us to have children, Ronan and Luc can't take part." Guilt twinged through her. She didn't like the idea of them not being part of this. It was one of the reasons she was certain she didn't want to conceive a child from this. It would be wrong to have any idea of which of her men was and wasn't the father.

"Are you suggesting we defeat the god with sex?" Jared raised an eyebrow.

"I didn't think you'd be the one complaining about that," Izban countered.

"Oh, I'm not. This is my *favourite* kind of plan." His grin widened, enjoyment in his eyes.

"But this is sex for a purpose," Macey pointed out. "If he's in the jar, he won't be able to get out and trigger the egg, right?" she asked Luc.

"I have no idea. I'm not sure how it works. But I'm sure we can put the jar somewhere it won't be found."

She nodded. It was as much of a plan as they were going to manage, especially when they didn't have all the facts. And if Eros showing up while they'd been visiting Nessie was anything to go by, then they had no chance of getting any of them.

"But I want to make one thing clear," she said, looking between the men. "No one is to get pregnant, is that understood?"

They each nodded in turn. No doubt her men felt the same way she did about knowing who fathered the child, and Izban had already made his feelings on the matter clear.

"Will my snake be okay?" Amber whispered.

Macey grimaced. She hadn't even considered that,

and she should have. Her friend had bonded with the creature, and she didn't want to see her hurt by it dying.

"We'll do everything we possibly can to make sure it is," she promised her best friend, knowing that every word of that was true. There was no way she was going to let Amber's pet get hurt if she could help it.

Jared clapped his hands together with glee. "This is the favourite plan of ours we've ever hatched."

Macey snorted. Of course it was. Jared could be very one-track minded when it came to certain things. Well, *one* thing.

Before they left Paris, they stopped at Jared's favourite patisserie. His excuse was that a meringue or two might bribe Eros to give them more time, but she didn't complain. She loved the strawberry tarts they made there. The perfect aphrodisiac. She clenched her thighs at the thought of what was to come. Having sex with three guys was a strange way of saving the world. But she wasn't going to complain. Much better than blood, sweat and tears. Except that it was most certainly going to get sweaty.

"Mademoiselle, are you all right?"

A woman next to them looked at her in concern.

Macey took a moment to realise that not only had she crossed her legs as if she urgently needed to pee, but she also had a wide smile on her face.

She nodded and followed the guys out of the patisserie, accompanied by the woman muttering something about drugs.

Izban and Amber were already waiting outside, him nibbling on a croissant, her telling him to put it back in the bag until later. Macey grinned. The two of them were behaving like an old married couple already. Not that she was any different when it came to her guys. From time to time, she still felt like a love-struck teenager having her first crush, over and over again.

Jared, who knew this area the best, led them into an abandoned alleyway to give them some privacy. Just before Macey could call the Staran, a figure appeared out of nowhere, blazing with golden light. Eros had found them.

Considering he'd probably been rejuvenated by what her mother and the three young men had done, he didn't look too happy. He had several large scratches on his chest, as if someone had scratched him in the heat of the moment. Macey didn't want to dwell on it too much. Her mother's sex life wasn't something she needed to know much about. Eros already had his bow in his hands and notched an arrow as soon as he spotted them, aiming it right at Macey.

"Hey," she greeted him innocently. "We were just about to return to our house to get started with the baby making."

Eros frowned, but didn't lower his bow. "You broke your promise."

"No, I didn't. I never said we'd jump into bed right away. How did you know we're the Wardens anyway?"

"I knew as soon as I stepped out of my egg. Knowledge infused me, preparing me for this world. I now know the pitiful state of humanity. I'm not surprised I was sent here for a new creation. It's time for a new beginning."

"Yeah, ehm, well, let's not start with the creating until we've had a chance to fulfil our promise, okay?"

Very slowly, Eros nodded and put the arrow back into his quiver. "I will watch."

"No, you won't," Amber protested. "No way am I going to have sex in front of a god."

Macey couldn't help but chuckle at those words. Yet another sentence she never thought she'd hear.

"I will watch," Eros repeated.

"You can watch me," Luc volunteered.

Ronan raised his hand like an oversized schoolboy. "And me."

It pained Macey to know that those two weren't going to be part of their fake baby making sex, but she'd make it up to them later. It didn't really matter, she told herself. They didn't always share the bed all at the same time. Sometimes, it was just one, or two, or three of the guys. Rarely four, though, because that felt like making one of them the odd one out. That only happened when one of the men was away.

"Agreed," Eros said, likely assuming that Luc and Ronan would be sleeping with Macey. He was in for a surprise. Maybe they could occupy him with card games or whatever gods did for fun. Maybe an archery lesson. Or Luc and Eros could compare their wings and do a bit of a competition in who had the prettiest feathers.

"You shall begin now," the god announced and without warning, golden light engulfed them, swallowing them whole.

It was nothing like travelling on the Staran. No gentle, welcoming embrace of the mythical pathways. No aniseed smell. One second, they were in the middle of Paris, the next, they were in their living room, standing around the now broken egg. The snake, curled up around the shards, hissed and flicked out its tongue. Amber smiled and picked it up, letting it curl around her wrist again.

"That snake is not coming into our bed," Izban warned. "I want neither a god nor a snake watching us."

Amber rolled her eyes. "I knew you were going to say that."

"Good. That means we understand each other."

For once, Macey agreed with Izban - and that didn't happen very often. She'd be creeped out by having a snake in her bedroom too, especially one that had been bound to a god in a weird and mysterious way. Who knew if he'd be able to watch through the snake's eyes.

Eros spread his arms and smiled at them. "You may begin."

Macey rolled her eyes. Was that god seriously giving them permission to have sex? This was all beginning to feel very surreal. No, correction, it had been surreal ever since they'd found out what that egg was. Or how nobody could remember where it had come from, not even the guy Izban had bought the egg from.

"Eros, you can come with me," Luc said and ushered the god out of the room, followed by Ronan.

"Know that I will be aware of what you're doing," Eros warned before he stepped through the door. "And your lives will be forfeit should you not adhere to our deal. Along with half the population of Earth."

Macey swallowed hard. Half the population? That was new. She took a deep breath and looked at the other Wardens.

"Let's do this."

8

It was hard not to think about the potential consequences of this. It had been a long time since she'd had sex in the small quiet moments while saving the world, and she'd never *had* to do it for that reason before. She knew all she had to do was relax and let her body take over the work. It wasn't like sleeping with her men was hard work.

Well, that wasn't true. It *was* hard in some ways. Three ways, to be exact. She snorted at the thought.

"You know, you're not supposed to laugh at naked men," Flint supplied.

"You're not naked yet," she pointed out.

Cam wrapped his arms around her from behind and pulled her against his chest. "You know you don't have to be nervous, right?"

Macey sighed. "I'm not nervous. We've done this hundreds of times." Probably. She hadn't *actually* kept count, that would have been weird. "I'm just..."

"Thinking too hard about the reason we're doing this," Cam finished for her.

She nodded and bit her lip, looking between the three other Wardens. It was a long time since these three men had kidnapped her. Or *saved* her. It depended which of them was telling the story, and how generous she was feeling. She'd done a lot of the saving herself over the years.

"Would it help if I send some incubus-y goodness your way?" Jared suggested.

Macey nodded without hesitation. Normally, she didn't need Jared's interference to get everything going, and simply enjoyed it once they were having fun. But right now, she was overthinking what she was supposed to be doing, and it was freaking her out a little.

"Come here then, little kelpie." He gestured for her to walk towards him.

The moment she stepped out of Cam's embrace, she missed his touch. That was always the case for her, but just like always, there were other men there to catch her. She closed the gap between her and the incubus, already feeling his magic wash over her.

By the time she reached him, she was feeling more relaxed.

Jared pulled her close and pressed his lips against hers in a searing kiss. She melted into him, letting the magic wash over him. After a moment he pulled away and brought his mouth level with her ear.

"I won't let it happen," he promised in a whisper.

Macey nodded. There was nothing else they could say

about the subject with Eros so close by. Luc and Ronan might be distracting him, but Macey was under no illusions that he was still listening and sensing them. In fact, she suspected he had powers that resembled those Jared used, and her incubus had a knack for sensing when people were being intimate. He'd used it to freak Amber and Izban out on several occasions, much to Macey's amusement.

"You're thinking too hard, little kelpie," Jared said.

"We can do something about that," Flint promised.

Jared gently turned her in his arms. The moment she was facing her other two Wardens, she noticed they'd already shed their clothes. Within moments, Jared's deft fingers were undoing the buttons on her shirt. She helped him undress her. Now wasn't the time for a slow and sensual disrobing experience. It was more important that she felt comfortable, and once her men started paying attention to her body, she knew she wouldn't be thinking of anything other than them. It would be a welcome distraction.

Cam held out his hand, and she took it. He gave her a gentle tug, then spun her around so she landed on the bed. Despite the seriousness of the situation, a small giggle escaped her. This was normal. Comfortable even. She was sure that their bodies would change as the years passed, but she'd still feel beautiful when they looked at her.

Flint climbed onto the bed beside her, then pressed a kiss against her lips as Cam pushed her legs apart.

Heat flooded through her. She squirmed under him as he began to trail his lips up the inside of her calf and up to her thigh. He licked and sucked as he went, and she knew what was going to happen next.

The worrying thoughts fled from her mind as she gave herself over to the sensations her men brought out in her. Flint broke their kiss and moved down to her breasts, stopping to nip at the soft skin of her throat as he did.

Macey let out a loud moan. It was both too much and not enough at the same time.

"Please," she demanded, not too sure what she was asking for.

Instead of giving her more, both Flint and Cam pulled away. She reached out for them, but Flint shook his head.

"You know that's not how it works when there's three of us," he said, amusement in his tone.

Another wave of desire crashed over her. She *did* know that.

She glanced over at Jared, waiting for him to take the lead. There were advantages to counting a sex demon among her lovers.

He stalked over to the bed, his now naked body glistening in the light.

She sat up properly and wetted her lips as she watched him. He reached out and cupped her cheek in his hand. "Are you ready to take everything we have to give, little kelpie?"

Macey's mouth went dry. "Always," she vowed, meaning it with every fibre of her being. There was never any doubt about how much she wanted them.

"Then get onto the bed," he instructed, a promise swinging in his voice.

She nodded, and did what he said, knowing he meant for her to get on all fours. It was one of the ways she could make the most of having three of them in the bed with her at the same time.

Cam moved around to the other side of the bed and stood at the side of it, his hard cock ready for her. She licked her lips, then leaned forward, taking it in her mouth with practised ease. Cam moaned and threaded his fingers into her hair.

She was only able to focus on what she was doing for a moment, as Flint's tongue found her clit. Without meaning to, Macey let out a small groan, vibrating Cam's cock in the process and causing his grip on her hair to tighten. She loved it when one of her men did that. It was easy to tell how much they were enjoying themselves.

Pleasure coiled tighter and tighter within her as Flint flicked his tongue with lightning precision. One of his hands rested on the curve of her leg as it met her ass as he did. She shuddered at the idea of what might be to come and resisted the urge to let go and enjoy her release. She knew if she held off, it would be more powerful when it came.

She felt Flint shift slightly, from where he was lying with his head under her, no doubt so he could make way for Jared. They'd done a lot of experimenting in order to get this position right, and if she opened her eyes, she'd have been able to see Flint's hard body lying to the side, exposed so that Jared had space behind her.

Flint probably had a hand on his own cock too, and stroked it as he pleasured her.

Another moan rumbled through the back of her throat at the thought. She loved watching them pleasure themselves.

As if summoned by her thoughts, Jared's hands began to roam over her ass, brushing past her opening as he did. She was almost certain he got hit by Flint's tongue as he did, but the other man didn't falter. While it was clear her men weren't into one another like that, she was grateful they were comfortable with the occasional accidental touch. It made her all the hotter just thinking about it.

Jared's fingers slipped into her and she stilled, using all the will power she had not to come before he was properly inside her. There was no doubt in her mind that it was going to be an explosive orgasm when she did let go, and she wanted to hold off as long as possible, it would only make it better.

Flint pulled away, but didn't move. No doubt he'd worked out how close she was to coming, and decided he was going to give her a moment to cool off first. She appreciated that.

Cam tugged on her hair, reminding her that she was supposed to be giving him the attention he deserved. She pressed her tongue against the underside of his cock, and got a loud moan from him for her troubles.

Jared replaced his fingers with his cock and pushed into her, rocking her forward into Cam. She moaned, as did the guys. She'd long since lost who was making what noises. It hardly mattered compared to the amazing sensations she was experiencing from all of them.

Flint's tongue darted out to press against her clit once more, just as Jared began to move inside her. Cam took control too, setting the tempo with which she took him into her mouth.

It was just as well. She'd lost all ability to control her body, and the pleasure coiled up inside her, determined to get out. She pushed back against it, all of her concentration going onto holding back her explosion. Macey couldn't tell which of her men was doing what, not that it mattered. This was about how they all felt. And with Jared being the one inside her, they could be certain not to give into Eros' real demands. As an incubus, he was sterile unless he decided he wanted to father a child. There would have been a lot of incubus children in the world otherwise.

Thought fled from her mind, and it became impossible to hold back any longer. Her whole body shook and she cried out, pushing back against Jared. At least, she thought she did. She wasn't in control of her body anymore.

Groans came from her men, and she was certain they were coming too, but she wasn't able to make out anything specific as a state of bliss settled over her.

After a moment or two, she opened her eyes, and found herself lying back on the bed between the three men. She didn't even remember them all collapsing.

"Hey," Flint said from beside her.

"Hi," she whispered, her voice hoarse.

"We can go again if you want," he suggested, most likely because he hadn't been able to have her in the same way the other had.

Macey was tempted to say yes, though she needed a little longer to recover. But she knew they couldn't.

She shook her head. "I'll take you up on that later," she promised. "But first, we need to go sort out Eros."

Jared chuckled. "You're thinking about him already? And here was me thinking we'd done a *good* job at distracting you."

A slow smile crept over Macey's face. "You did an excellent job at distracting me," she vowed. "But saving the world comes before our sex life."

Cam snorted. "Except when saving the world is *part* of it."

A small giggle escaped without Macey meaning it to. "This is one of the stranger things we've done to save the world."

Cam shuffled on the bed, propping himself up so he could see her better. "You think *this* is the strangest thing you've done to save the world?"

Macey moved back to prop herself up against the pillows. "Isn't it?"

"You killed an illusion of yourself once," Flint supplied.

"Oh and let's not forget you had a seelie living inside you for a bit," Jared added.

"And you became the Empress of the sea kelpies..." Flint started.

Macey held up a finger. "That wasn't to save the world. *Technically,* that was my birthright."

"That you happened to find out about while saving the world," he countered.

She shook her head in bemusement. "If you're going to use that logic, then we've engaged in a lot of sex to save the world, not just tonight, but the other ones too."

"If you're not careful, I'm going to convince you to carry on doing the saving," Jared teased. "I can live with sex to save the world."

"You're just happy so long as you have sex," Macey pointed out. "But we should go check on the others and see how they're getting on with Eros." She hoped Ronan and Luc were all right. It sucked that they hadn't been able to join in this part of the plan, though she'd make it up to them later.

9

Macey ached for a shower, but instead she put on a robe and waited for her guys to put on some trousers. She wanted them all to look like they'd just come out of bed, to make it even more obvious for Eros that they'd fulfilled their part of the bargain.

"Amber and Izban have finished too," Jared said, making Macey cringe a little. As much as Amber and her liked to compare notes in their girl chats, she didn't want to think of her best friend having sex when she'd just come from bed herself.

"Let's deal with Eros," she said with a sigh. "I hope the others have kept him occupied."

She led them to the living room, expecting the three men - well, two men and a god - to sit there, maybe in silence, or maybe in conversation. Instead, Eros was on his knees in between Luc and Ronan, his hands bound behind his back, a scarf in his mouth to stop him from speaking. She couldn't believe her eyes. Why the waves were they doing this to the god?

"What the fuck is going on here?" Macey asked, storming into the room.

"Did you have fun?" Ronan asked innocently, pretending not to know what she was talking about.

"Speak. Now. Why is there a naked god tied up in our living room?"

"There isn't," Luc replied darkly. "Is there, *Eros*?"

He emphasised the god's name with distaste.

"Hhhmpffh."

Luc glared at him. "Sorry, I didn't get that."

"Have a seat," Ronan invited them, a happy grin on his face. He was the complete opposite to Luc's anger and surliness.

Macey sighed and sat down, with the other three squeezing onto the sofa on both sides. Cam took her hand and squeezed it reassuringly, while looking just as worried and confused as her.

"While you were having fun," Ronan began, "we noticed a change in our friend here. Luc used his magic to block all sound from the bedrooms, so he shouldn't have been able to hear that you'd started, but he obviously knew."

"It was very obvious," Luc growled, pointing at the god's naked crotch. "I thought that thing would blow up like a balloon."

Macey choked. She really didn't want to look at Eros's giant cock again, but she couldn't help it. He was still mostly erect, and waves, no woman would ever be able to accommodate that. He'd tear her in half.

"So we were wondering if that's a god thing," Ronan

continued. "Since he's the God of Love and all that. But then his scratches started to heal."

Macey's gaze flew to the god's chest. Earlier, there had been several long scratch marks there. Now, they were gone. Divine healing powers?

"As if he was using the sexual energy you were producing to heal himself. Now, I've don't know much about Eros, but I do know that incubi can do that. Right, Jared?"

"Right. It's a nifty trick."

Ronan nodded. "Very. Wish I had that skill. But anyway, that made us suspicious. Why hadn't he healed those scratches earlier? Surely, a powerful god like Eros should be able to deal with such minor wounds, right? So we conducted a little experiment."

Macey was getting impatient, and it seemed that so was Eros. He fought against his restraint and tried to talk through the scarf, but neither Luc nor Ronan seemed inclined to let him speak.

"Hurry up," she said, "what did you do to him?"

A small smile appeared on Luc's lips. "I asked the house to create an accident that would put Eros in danger. Something that would make him show his powers. The house, amazing as it is, dropped the chandelier on him."

The walls shook softly, as if the house was laughing. Macey couldn't help but grin. She loved this place. She'd give the walls a little pat later on to thank it for its assistance.

"Of course, nothing happened," Ronan said triumphantly. "Luc had to use his magic to stop the chandelier from crushing Eros. That's when we decided that it was safe to tie him up and ask him a few pointed questions." He nodded towards the bow and quiver of arrows in a corner. "Turns out he's not powerful at all without his magic weapons."

Jared leaned forward. "So you're saying he's just a simple incubus?"

"Not simple," Luc interjected. "He's pretty strong, and, most of all, he's both cunning and twisted. But he's no danger without his weapons and with my magic neutralising his incubus powers. He won't be trying to seduce you anytime soon."

Macey was glad Luc had trained with Jared a couple of months ago - mostly because both of them had been bored - to see whether he could withstand the incubus's magic. They'd discovered that not only could Luc do that, but he could also prevent Jared from using his talents in the first place. The daimon had promised never to use that power on Jared unless it was a matter of life or death, but it certainly came in handy in this instance.

"So how did he get into the egg?" Flint asked before Macey could pose the same question. "And how is the snake connected to it all?"

"We think we've figured it out," Luc said, "but you were back before we could start the interrogation properly. And we thought you'd quite like to do this yourself."

Macey smiled grimly. "You're right about that. Ronan, could you get Amber and Izban and fill them in on everything? They should be done."

She shot Jared a questioning look, just in case the couple had decided on a round two, but the incubus nodded.

"Please wait for me if you decide to torture him," Ronan said before he left the room. "I really want to witness that."

Eros's golden eyes widened slightly.

"Why is he golden?" Macey asked. "He doesn't look like a normal incubus."

"Hhhhhmpfffhhh."

She raised her eyebrows at Eros. "Yes?"

"Hhmmmmmmmmfffffm."

"I can sense some ancient magic around him," Luc said slowly. "I thought it was a god thing, but now that we've pretty much established that he's not a god, I think it might be a spell, a kind of glamour that conceals his true form. Magic that old would usually be bound in some kind of artifact, but he's not wearing any jewellery that could be enchanted."

Macey got up and walked straight to the bow in the corner. Without thinking, she took the bow and snapped it in half.

Her men's gasp made her swirl around. Eros no longer looked like Eros.

His golden skin had turned pale and sickly looking, his hair was now grey with white streaks, his wings had disappeared, while his cock had shrunk to the size of a shrivelled banana. A very small, dusty banana. Nausea rose up in Macey. She'd found that man attractive? He looked five times her age, at least, and close to death's door. Wrinkles and liver spots covered his skin, empha-sising his age.

"What the fuck," Cam cursed. "What just happened?"

"Say hello to the true Eros," Macey announced weakly. "If that is even his name."

Eros looked shell-shocked, his eyes darting around the room as if looking for an escape. No way was she going to let him get away. He'd threatened her, made a fool of her, and forced her to consider having a child she didn't want yet. He was going to pay.

The door opened, followed by Izban's shriek. Both him and Amber stared at the tied-up man, but while he looked surprised, Amber's face was a mask of fury.

"Can I torture him?" she asked and marched up to Eros, glaring down at him. "I promise I will make it hurt."

Eros shied away from her, but he seemed too weak to move much. His legs weren't tied, so he could have got up, but along with his glamour all his strength had been sapped from him. Macey almost pitied him, but then she reminded himself of what he'd done.

"Go ahead," she said generously, nodding at Amber. "But leave his tongue intact, we want him to be able to answer our questions."

Amber glowered at the fake god. "You were supposed to be a dragon. A cute little dragon pet."

Jared snorted with amusement. "That's what you're angry about?"

She ignored him. "Was the snake real at least?"

Eros looked at her with wide, bloodshot eyes, then

shook his head, almost with regret. Amber's disappointment filled the room like a physical manifestation of her emotion. Macey ached for her friend. While she hadn't been the biggest fan of the snake herself, it had been obvious how much Amber had liked the reptile.

"I'll get you another one," Izban whispered. "Or a real dragon egg. I'll make sure it's an actual dragon, this time. No more orphic eggs."

Amber nodded but didn't take her eyes off Eros. "I'm going to remove the scarf, but if you say something I don't like, I'll stuff it down your throat, understood?"

Eros inclined his head in resigned acceptance. He was a broken man, that much was obvious. None of his previous arrogance remained.

Amber untied the scarf not too gently, revealing the man's stubbly chin and yellow teeth. Yuck. He clearly had never heard of brushing his teeth. Macey really hoped Nessie hadn't slept with Eros. Hopefully, her three young men had been enough, and all Eros had done was hit her with an arrow. That was bad enough. If she hadn't broken the bow, she'd use it to shoot an arrow at Eros herself, and not one made of love.

"Who are you?" Amber demanded sharply.

"Eros," the man replied in an unsteady voice.

"Are you kidding me? Did you not listen to me threaten you with unspeakable violence?"

He flinched. "My name really is Eros. But I'm not the god Eros. Just an incubus."

Ronan smiled in satisfaction, while Luc looked pleased. Macey was proud of her two men for figuring it all out.

"What's the story with the egg?" Amber asked. "How did you get inside? Where's the snake?"

"It was my prison," Eros muttered with a sigh. "I was trapped in there, like a genie in a bottle. The mage who imprisoned me spelled my confinement to look like an orphic egg, so that nobody would ever be tempted to open it. I would have advised against that, but it's not like he asked me."

"What were you imprisoned for?" Jared asked curiously.

Eros shrugged. "Various things. Murder. Inciting violence. Fraud. Rape. None of it was bad enough though to be held inside an egg for two hundred years."

Macey couldn't help herself, she pointed at Eros and a blast of icy water shot towards him, filling his mouth until his eyes bulged in fear.

"Hey, I'm the one in charge of interrogating him," Amber complained, but her smile belied her words. "But you better stop before this turns into water-boarding."

Amber was right. Macey pulled back her water magic and let Eros breathe again. He glared at her, but the defeat in his eyes was unmistakable. He was ready to tell them everything.

"How did you pull me into the egg?" Macey asked before Amber could pose the next question. "That doesn't seem like something an incubus should be able to do."

"The mage allowed me one visitor every century," Eros replied sullenly. "You were my first. The whole crap about me being three entities was just a lie. I'm good at lying."

"Yeah, I don't doubt that. But just a reminder, if you lie to us now, it won't end well for you."

Eros cringed. "I'm not lying, I promise."

"Was it a coincidence that Izban bought the egg?" Amber asked.

"No. Over time, my prison's walls weakened, and I was able to listen to some of the conversations going on around me. The guy who owned my egg really thought it was a dragon's. It took years, but eventually I was able to use my incubus powers to suggest he might want to sell it to the Wardens I'd heard so much about. I knew you'd saved the world and I was sure you'd do whatever it took to save it again. It all worked out even better than I expected."

"But why kids?" Macey interrupted. "What's that got to do with anything? And I assume that prophecy about our children having to be future Wardens was fake?"

"I can answer that one," Jared said softly. "For an incubus, there's nothing better than the kick you get from feeding on an orgasm that results in pregnancy. It lasts days, weeks even."

Eros licked his lips. "Exactly. And I knew it would be even more potent with several people, all of them supernaturals at that. It could have restored my strength to its previous level, but you cheated."

He had the audacity to look angry at that. Macey was very tempted to use her magic on him again. What an arse.

"What shall we do with him?" Luc sounded both annoyed and exasperated, exactly what Macey felt too.

"Kill him," Izban spat. "He's a murderer. I would have been fine with imprisoning him for centuries, but it seems that even a weird egg prison doesn't keep him locked up."

"No, we can't kill him," Macey argued. "That's not our way. We're Wardens, we protect life, we don't take it unless we absolutely have to. Killing someone in battle is very different from executing a prisoner."

"I agree," Amber said, although she was still glaring at Eros. "Jared, how strong is he now that he no longer has his glamour nor the bow?"

"Wait, how did you even get the bow?" Macey asked, turning to the fake god.

"I hid it in a magic pocket that's bigger on the inside. The mage who imprisoned me never knew about it. It was the only item I was able to take with me into the egg. Not that it did me any good. There were no being in that egg with me that I could have shot to feed on their sexual energy."

Macey shuddered at the thought of him hitting Nessie with one of those arrows. He'd fed on her mother. She was going to check on Nessie as soon as they were done here.

"He's pretty weak," Jared said. "Although that could change of course if he feeds a couple of times. I doubt anyone would let him close though with the way he looks now."

Luc stepped forward. "I might be able to lock his powers for good. He'd basically be human."

Eros's face turned into a mess of fear and hate. "Don't do that. I don't want to be stuck like this, looking like an old man. You could just as well kill me."

"You *are* an old man," Macey snapped. "And I think it's time you act your age and don't go around manipulating people. Luc, do it. Then we'll drop him off somewhere on Earth where he can't do any harm."

"The Antarctic is a lovely, empty place," Izban suggested with a cruel smile. "Or maybe the Saharan desert. Far away from the nearest oasis."

Amber walked over to her boyfriend and took his hand. "Don't be like that, Izzy. It doesn't suit you."

Macey suppressed a chuckle at hearing the ice mage being called Izzy. No matter how often Amber called him that, Macey would never get used to connecting the surly, constantly angry mage with that name. Amber had been good for him though, he actually smiled from time to time now.

Luc kneeled down in front of Eros and put his hands around the man's head. His black wings extended and wrapped themselves around the two of them, hiding them from view. Jared stepped forward and took Macey's hand, squeezing it reassuringly. She smiled up at the incubus as a feeling of warmth spread in her chest. The knot of anger unravelled, taking with it the hate she felt for Eros.

They all waited in silence while Luc worked his magic on the prisoner. It took several minutes, but he finally folded his wings on his back and got up. Eros looked just like before, except that he seemed even more defeated. Macey almost felt pity for him, but then she reminded herself of his crimes. He'd killed people. It was right that he was suffering for it.

"Maybe we should get him some clothes," she suggested. "I think we've all seen enough naked incubus for today."

Once they'd dressed him in a simple tracksuit, Macey and her guys took Eros into the Staran, while Amber and Izban stayed at home. The beithir was still sad about the loss of the snake, but Macey was sure that Izban would find a way to cheer his girlfriend up. He wasn't the most emotional of men, but he did have a hidden romantic streak.

Macey had asked the Staran to take them to London, where she'd planned to drop Eros at a homeless shelter, but of course, the Staran had other ideas. It spat them out in front of a very familiar house.

"Did you ask them to bring us to Malan's home?" Flint asked in confusion.

Macey shook her head. "It seems the Staran are doing their weird thing again. I guess there's a reason they brought us here."

"Come on in, the waffles are getting cold!" the headless prophet shouted from inside the house before they could even knock on the door.

Macey grinned at her men. "I love the Staran. We're finally getting some waffles. I think we've earned them."

Eros frowned. "What's so special about waffles?"

She shot him an exasperated look. How could this guy not like waffles? Not that she should be surprised. She bet serial killers like him preferred raw steaks and grilled fish with the heads still attached. She shuddered at the thought. There was a reason she was a vegetarian.

Malan's house looked as cosy as ever, and the smell of fresh waffles made Macey instantly feel at home. Now that their Warden life was over, she wasn't scared of Malan spouting new prophecies anymore. Life had become rather simple - excluding manipulating fake gods.

The bodiless prophet was in the kitchen, hovering over a mountain of waffles. "I see you've brought the servant I requested. Well done. I'm getting older and I could do with some help cleaning the house."

He gave Eros an innocent smile. Macey was sure the prophet knew exactly who Eros was and what he'd done. She wouldn't even be surprised if he knew the sorcerer who'd imprisoned the incubus in the first place.

"Servant?" Eros spluttered. "No way."

Macey grinned and pushed him towards Malan. "Don't complain. You'll have a roof over your head and no temptation that could make you re-offend. You can't kill Malan and you certainly can't use your incubus powers on him, should they return despite Luc's lock on them. It's perfect." She sat down and slid a waffle on her plate. "And we get paid for it in waffles. Win-win."

Malan laughed, surprising her. The prophet looked more relaxed than she'd ever seen him. "Take a seat, everyone. Not you, Eros. You have some windows to clean. And the toilet hasn't seen any bleach in a couple of decades."

Macey's men took a seat around her, their presence adding to the happiness she felt. This was the perfect moment. Waffles, her wonderful guys and the knowledge that Eros would never hurt anyone again. This quest had probably been the most unusual they'd done so far, but at least it had ended in waffles.

She poured maple syrup over her second waffle and stared at it lovingly. "Come to mama, baby."

Malan cleared his throat. "There is something you should know... about the role your future children will play in the fate of the world."

Macey choked on her waffle, then flung her fork at the prophet. Nobody would determine the destiny of her children. No one but her. She'd make sure of that. And with that thought, she grabbed Cam's fork and continued eating her waffles.

EPILOGUE

Many, many, many years later...

Macey paced back and forth, passing Izban as he did the same.

"Will the two of you stop, you're giving me a headache," Flint mumbled.

"She isn't back yet," Izban pointed out.

"She's a giant flying snake, she'll be fine," Jared added as he came back into the hallway and handed Cam a mug of tea.

Macey had tried to pry Izban away from the door and waiting for Amber earlier, but all that had happened was that he'd worried her so much that she'd joined him. Her men hadn't been impressed, especially since it meant they'd have to put the twins to bed.

"You don't know that," Macey countered. "Weird things have happened to us during storms..."

Luc came up to her and wrapped his arms around her, pulling her close. "Nothing like that has happened in decades, she's perfectly safe. Beithirs have been doing things this way for centuries."

She pursed her lips, but leaned into him even so. He had a point. They hadn't had to save the world since the odd attempt of the trapped incubus pretending to be Eros.

"I don't like it," Macey insisted. "She said she'd be back in an hour."

"She probably didn't count on how long it would take to fly back with a youngling." Flint flashed her a reassuring smile.

"I thought we'd been through this, they're just kids, not younglings," Ronan told the Fire Warden.

Flint shrugged. "Younglings sounds cooler."

"And what are you calling yourself that's cooler than Dad?" Jared teased.

Flint's expression grew serious. "There's nothing cooler than being called Dad."

Macey's heart swelled at the words, like they always did when one of her men talked about being a father.

"Mama?" a small voice called, as if summoned by her thoughts.

Luc let go of her as she pulled away to go see to the small boy wandering down the corridor on stubby two-year-old feet.

"Dillon? Why are you out of bed?" she asked, scooping down and picking her up her son.

He wrapped his arms around her and snuggled into her shoulder.

"Mama say night?" he asked.

She closed her eyes and smiled, kissing the top of his head.

"I'm waiting for Auntie Amber to get back," she told him, even though he probably didn't understand.

The little boy pulled back, then nodded gravely. She wasn't sure if he knew what was going on, or that he was going to get a new playmate soon.

"Is your brother still awake?" she asked him, rocking from side to side in an attempt to soothe him. He probably didn't need it, but it seemed to be an automatic reaction for her.

He nodded again.

Macey sighed. No one had prepared her for how difficult it was to get two-year-olds to sleep at the right time. Though she supposed it was hard to tell what part of the day it was outside when they lived in the house in the mists. Things would change when they were old enough to go to school in the loch.

So long as they could shift, that was. For some reason, Macey had been reluctant to keep them in the water for long enough to find out yet, though her twins both liked splashing their feet in the shallow ends of the house's pool.

"Why don't you go to Papa and I'll go get your brother," she said, handing him to Cam.

Dillon instantly snuggled into his father's shoulder. Macey had no idea which of her men was the twins' biological father, or even if they had the same one, as they weren't identical. But it didn't matter. Each of them was as caring and protective of the two boys as each other. They were fantastic parents.

She padded down the corridor and to the boys' room. She was sure that they would want separate bedrooms, and when they did, the house would accommodate. But for now, it was easier to have the two of them in the same place.

Unbidden, Macey touched her stomach. Change was coming soon, that was for certain.

Carwyn sat up in his cot, his huge dark eyes staring up at her. He was already the shier of the two children, though Macey suspected he'd make up for it in intelligence.

She reached in and picked him up, her heart fluttering as he grabbed onto her, not unlike his brother had. She'd resisted motherhood for so long, thinking she wouldn't be very good at it. And then she'd had the boys. It had been nothing like she'd expected, but she'd loved every moment of it. All the late nights, painful moments, and tears were worth it for one smile, or one of them touching her cheek with their hand.

It only took her a few steps to get back to where the others were waiting for Amber.

"Is she back?" she asked, even though she could tell that the beithir hadn't returned yet.

Izban shook her head. "I should go find her..." He stepped towards the door, only for it to fling open and reveal Macey's best friend framed by flashing lightning.

"Did you bring the storm back with you again?" Cam asked with a sigh, cradling Dillon's head so he didn't get too scared. The twins didn't particularly like lightning, much to Amber's dismay.

"It followed me," Amber said.

Izban rushed over to her and stared down at the bundle in Amber's arms.

"It's beautiful," he said.

"She," Amber corrected. "We have a daughter."

"A daughter," he whispered. "The dragon is going to be so jealous."

"You could use it as a guard dragon," Macey pointed out, moving closer so she could see her best friend's baby.

"That's a great idea," Amber responded, her eyes lighting up as she did. "Our little Ingrid will never have to worry about the boys pulling her tail with a guard dragon around." At that, the beithir's own tail wrapped around her waist, as if remembering the times when it had been pulled off by bullies while Amber had been at Ben Vair.

"I don't think she'll have to worry about anyone pulling at her hair or her tail when she has Dillon and Carwyn watching out for her," Jared said proudly.

"Especially not with your other little one on the way," Amber said offhandedly.

All five of Macey's men turned to look at her, confusion in their eyes.

"Another?" Flint asked.

"Oh, yes. Did I forget to tell you..." Macey flashed them the most innocent eyes she could manage, glad she was holding one of the twins so Luc wouldn't pick her up and spin her around like he had when he'd found out about the twins.

"Are you serious?" Ronan asked.

She nodded. "We'll be welcoming another little one soon."

Amber sighed happily. "Two happy families under one roof, neither having to save the world."

Macey smiled. As glad as she was for the things they'd all been through after it had brought them all together, she was also pleased that her children wouldn't have to save the world the way they did.

Probably.

She looked around the room at the people she cared about most in the whole world and breathed an easy sigh of relief. This was going to be her life for a long time to come, and if that was the case, then she'd be the happiest kelpie in the world.

THE END

Thank you for reading *Inside the Egg!* If you enjoyed the story, we'd love it if you could take a moment to write a review. They're like waffles for us.

If you haven't read the other books about Macey's journey yet, you can start with *From the Deeps* or the *Seven Wardens box set* (combining books 1-4).

And if you'd like to stay up to date with this series and other books, subscribe to our newsletters:
authorlauragreenwood.co.uk/p/mailing-list-sign-up
skyemackinnon.com/newsletter

ABOUT SKYE MACKINNON

Skye MacKinnon is a USA Today & International Bestselling Author whose books are filled with strong heroines who don't have to choose.

She embraces her Scottishness with fantastical Scottish settings and a dash of mythology, no matter if she's writing about Celtic gods, cat shifters, or the streets of Edinburgh.

When she's not typing away at her favourite cafe, Skye loves dried mango, as much exotic tea as she can squeeze into her cupboards, and being covered in pet hair by her demon cat Sootie.

Subscribe to her newsletter:
skyemackinnon.com/newsletter

Join her Facebook group:
facebook.com/groups/skyesbookharem

facebook.com/skyemackinnonauthor

twitter.com/skye_mackinnon

instagram.com/skyemackinnonauthor

bookbub.com/authors/skye-mackinnon

goodreads.com/SkyeMacKinnon

amazon.com/author/skye_mackinnon

ABOUT LAURA GREENWOOD

Laura is a USA Today Bestselling Author of paranormal, fantasy, and urban fantasy romance (though she can occasionally be found writing contemporary romance). When she's not writing, she drinks a lot of tea, tries to resist French macarons, and works towards a diploma in Egyptology. She lives in the UK, where most of her books are set.

Follow the Author

- Website: www.authorlauragreenwood.co.uk
- Mailing List: www.authorlauragreenwood.co.uk/p/mailing-list-sign-up.html
- Facebook Group: http://facebook.com/groups/theparanormalcouncil
- Facebook Page: http://facebook.com/authorlauragreenwood
- Bookbub: www.bookbub.com/authors/laura-greenwood

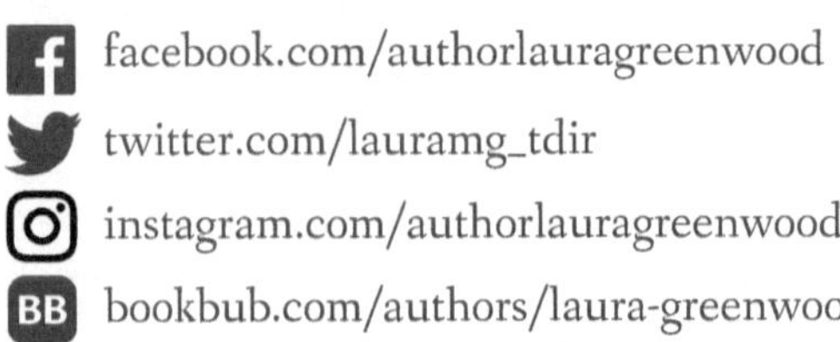
facebook.com/authorlauragreenwood
twitter.com/lauramg_tdir
instagram.com/authorlauragreenwood
bookbub.com/authors/laura-greenwood
amazon.com/author/lauragreenwood